This book belongs to

SEPTEMBER

Christmas 2010

© 2010 by Parragon Books Ltd
This 2010 edition published by Sandy Creek,
by arrangement with Parragon.

Sandy Creek
122 Fifth Avenue
New York, NY 10011

ISBN 978-1-4351-2760-9

10 9 8 7 6 5 4 3 2 1 Lot
Manufactured 4/19/2010
Printed in China

The Perfect Snowflake

One morning, Emma woke up to find
something magical happening outside
her bedroom window.

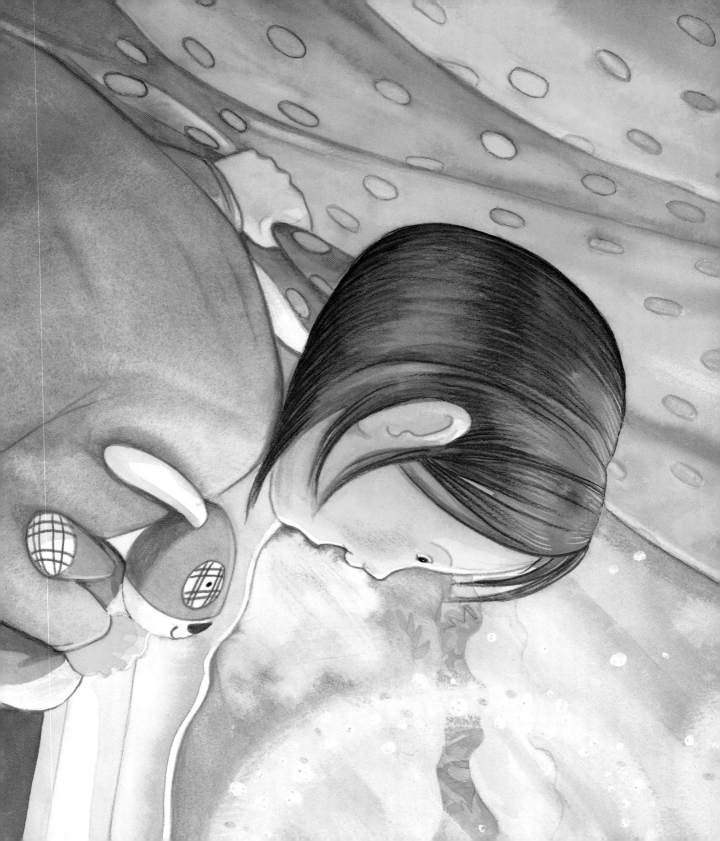

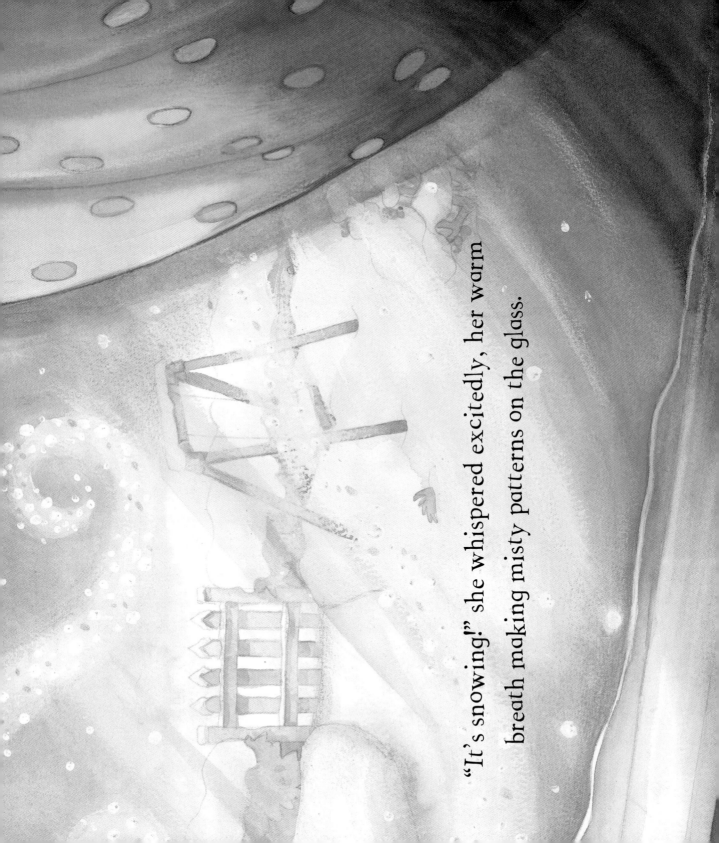

"It's snowing!" she whispered excitedly, her warm breath making misty patterns on the glass.

Outside, snowflakes

swirled and twirled.

in the air before floating to the ground.

Emma had never seen anything so beautiful. "If only I could have a snowflake of my own to keep!" she thought.

In the yard, Emma caught lots of snowflakes, but each one disappeared when she tried to show Mommy.

"Snowflakes melt when they're warm," Mommy explained.

"But I wanted to keep one!" Emma sighed.

Later that day, the sun shone just as the last few snowflakes fell. They shimmered in the light like sparkly diamonds, before vanishing onto the ground.

That afternoon, Mommy showed Emma
how to make a paper snowflake.

"It's not the same as having a REAL
snowflake," Emma sighed, remembering
what it was like to play in the snow.

"REAL snowflakes dance in the sky."

"REAL snowflakes sparkle in the sun."

"REAL snowflakes dazzle like diamonds in the snow!"

Emma couldn't wait to play with REAL snowflakes again.

But the next morning, when Emma went outside to play, all the snow had melted.

Just then, the most perfect snowflake Emma had ever seen fluttered in the sky.

This snowflake danced in the sky...

sparkled in the sun, and... **dazzled** like a diamond.

But this snowflake wasn't real. It was made of paper, with sparkly sequins and glitter sprinkled on top.

Emma hugged Mommy.
"This snowflake is
definitely one I can keep,"
she grinned.

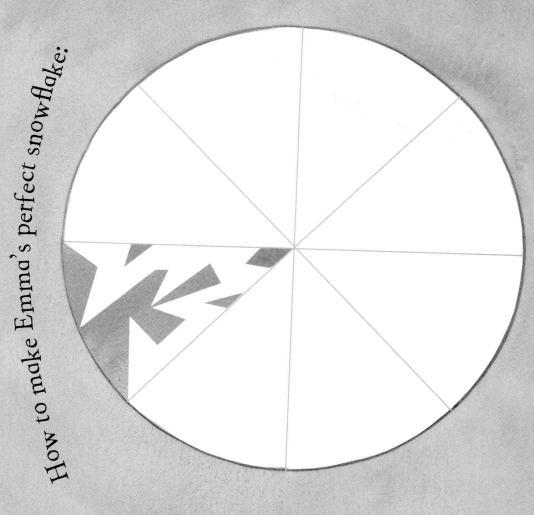

How to make Emma's perfect snowflake:

Copy the above pattern onto paper. Ask a grown up to help you cut out the circle, then fold on the lines, and cut away the purple areas to reveal your snowflake.